This book belongs to:

_____

5-Minute Stories

Written by
Liza Baker and Lara Bergen

Illustrated by
the Disney Storybook Artists and Robin Cuddy

DISNEY **PRESS**

New York

Printed in China

First Edition

10 9 8 7 6 5 4 3 2 1

Library of Congress Card Catalog Number on file.
ISBN 978-1-4231-3048-2

G942-9090-6-09349

SUSTAINABLE
FORESTRY
INITIATIVE

Certified Fiber Sourcing

www.sfiprogram.org

PWC-SFICOC-260
For Text Paper Only

Contents

Beauty and the Beast

The Sleigh Ride

Long ago, an enchantress cast a spell on a castle. She transformed the handsome young prince into a hideous beast and his servants into household objects.

"Just look at me," grumbled the Beast. "I've been so cruel, holding Belle captive in my castle. How will she ever see me as anything but a monster?"

"Come now," said Mrs. Potts gently. "All you have to do is show her what is inside your heart."

"You must act like a gentleman!" Lumiere the candelabrum chimed in. "Be romantic. Compliment her. And most of all, be kind, gentle, and sincere!"

"And don't be so grumpy!" added Chip, Mrs. Potts's young son.

Mrs. Potts gave her son a stern look. But they all knew Chip was right.

"I have an idea!" said the Beast, smiling. "Why don't I invite Belle to go on a sleigh ride? It just snowed outside, and she might like the fresh air."

"Perfect!" said Lumiere.

"A wonderful idea," agreed Mrs. Potts.

"Very romantic," added Chip.

"That's enough out of you," Mrs. Potts said to Chip, trying not to smirk.

The Beast sent Lumiere to extend his invitation.

"That sounds lovely!" said Belle. "I've been stuck in this castle far too long."

Belle ran down the long staircase and stepped outside. Glimmering white snowflakes fell from the sky. It was a perfect winter day.

Just then, the Beast pulled up in a gleaming horse-drawn sleigh.

"How beautiful!" exclaimed Belle.

The Beast smiled as he took her hand and helped her into the sleigh. He didn't mention that he had spent all morning polishing it just for her. Once she was settled, he covered her with a warm blanket.

They took off across the powdery snow. Belle laughed happily as the Beast guided the sleigh through the forest path. Soon they came to a clearing in the woods. Before them was a frozen pond. The Beast pulled on the reins and stopped at the edge of the pond.

"This is such a magical place," said Belle. "How did you ever find it?"

"I used to come here long ago," said the Beast. "It was one of my favorite places. I wanted to . . . um . . . share it with you."

Then the Beast took out a picnic basket filled with hot chocolate, cookies, bread, and fruit.

When they had finished their meal, the Beast asked Belle if she wanted to ice-skate.

"Oh, yes," she replied. "Father and I used to go every winter. I love ice-skating!"

Soon Belle was spinning effortlessly across the pond's smooth surface. The Beast was less graceful. Hitting a bump in the ice, he lost his balance and toppled to the ground. At first he was angry, but then he saw Belle looking at him kindly. Remembering his friends' advice, he smiled as Belle helped him to his feet.

"Everyone falls sometimes," said Belle. "It's part of learning."

Before long, they were gliding across the ice arm in arm, enjoying each other's company in the crisp winter air.

They grew tired and decided to rest. Just then, a timid fawn wandered out of the forest.

"Poor thing," said Belle. "She looks scared and hungry." Taking an apple from their picnic basket, Belle showed the Beast how to gently feed the young deer.

Soon the sun was setting. It was time to go. As they made their way home, Belle thought about the day she had spent with the Beast. There was something different about him. He had shown Belle a kinder, softer side. Perhaps they could be friends, after all. . . .

Cinderella

The Dance Lesson

"Just imagine," said Cinderella excitedly. "There's a ball at the palace tonight in honor of the Prince. And every maiden in the land is invited. That means me, too!"

All of Cinderella's friends clapped and chirped as they gathered around. They loved their "Cinderelly."

"Oh, dear," said Cinderella with a sigh. "There is so much to do! I can only go if I finish my chores. And today, Stepmother has given me more work than ever. There is washing, mending, ironing, cooking, scrubbing, sweeping, and . . ."

Suddenly three loud shrieks came from downstairs.

"Cinderelllllaaaa! Come down here immediately, and help us get ready for the ball!" her stepsisters cried together.

Her cruel stepmother and stepsisters wouldn't give poor Cinderella any time to do the rest of her chores.

"Mend my dress!" screeched Anastasia.

"Polish my shoes!" whined Drizella.

"Iron my cloak!" demanded her stepmother.

Hours later, Cinderella began to sweep and scrub the endless stone floor.

Suddenly Jaq had an idea. "I know!" he said. "We help-a Cinderelly!"

All of the other mice nodded in agreement.

"What would I do without you!" said Cinderella, patting each of them on the head. "You are so good to me."

Everyone joined in the cleaning, singing happily as they went.

As she worked, Cinderella began to imagine the magical evening ahead. Everyone would be dressed in the finest clothes. Cinderella would wear her mother's beautiful gown. The ballroom would come alive with music, dancing, and laughter. The handsome young Prince would bow before Cinderella and ask her to dance.

Suddenly Cinderella stopped dreaming.

"Oh, no!" she cried. "I've never been to a ball. I don't even know how to dance!"

"Don't you worry, Cinderelly!" Jaq smiled reassuringly. "Us show you dance! Easy pie!"

With that, Jaq bowed before Perla and extended his hand. "Dance, please, missy?" he asked.

Perla blushed as she took Jaq's hand.

Gus was the conductor. He got all the birds to sing.

Jaq and Perla spun around and around, gliding across the floor.

Cinderella watched and then copied their movements.

"Just listen and move! See?" said Perla. "Not so scary."

Using her broom as an imaginary partner, Cinderella danced and twirled gracefully throughout the room. She led everyone across the floor, sweeping and cleaning as they went.

"Good-good, Cinderelly!" said Jaq, beaming. "Lucky Prince gets to dance with Cinderelly."

The mice collapsed on the floor, laughing.

"Thank you all so much," Cinderella told her friends. "With your help, tonight might be the night that all my dreams come true!"

THE LITTLE MERMAID

A Special Surprise

The underwater kingdom was quiet and peaceful. Every mermaid and merman was in bed fast asleep—everyone but Princess Ariel and her friend Flounder.

"Hurry up, Flounder!" cried Ariel. "It's almost time for the party. We can't be late!"

Trying not to make a sound, Ariel and Flounder swam away from King Triton's palace. They began their journey toward the surface.

"B-b-but, Ariel," said Flounder, "are you sure we should go to the surface? Remember the last time? Your father got so angry. You know how he feels about humans!"

"That's why this time, we can't get caught!" said Ariel, smiling. She wasn't going to let anything ruin her plans for tonight.

Eric, the prince Ariel had saved in a shipwreck, was having a royal ball. Ariel had a very special surprise for him.

"Swim faster, Flounder!" she cried, glancing back at him.

Flounder raced to keep up.

Just as Ariel and Flounder approached the surface, Ariel saw colorful lights dance across the water. When they poked their heads out of the water, Ariel and Flounder saw the lights explode in the air above Prince Eric's castle.

"I've never seen anything so beautiful in all my life," said Ariel breathlessly. "The human world is a wonderful place!"

"It sure is pretty!" said Flounder.

Off in the distance, Prince Eric stood on the palace balcony. He just didn't feel like joining in the royal celebration. He couldn't stop thinking about the mysterious girl with the lovely voice who had saved his life in the shipwreck. Why has she disappeared? he wondered.

Flounder spotted the prince first.

"Look, Ariel," he said, pointing a fin at the castle.

Ariel's heart leaped with joy when she saw Prince Eric.

"It's time for my surprise!" she said, winking at Flounder.

Swimming up to a nearby rock, Ariel and Flounder hid behind it.

"R-r-ready?" asked Flounder.

With a nod, Ariel closed her eyes, opened her mouth, and began to sing.

Suddenly, the night was filled with the sweet sound of Ariel's voice. She sang a song she had written just for Eric. It was Ariel's special gift to him.

Hearing her beautiful voice again, Eric's face lit up. "It can't be!" he said. "I must be hearing the sounds of the wind." Still, he remained on the balcony, enchanted by the beautiful song filling the night air.

When the song was over, Eric looked out across the sea. He hoped to catch a glimpse of the wonderful girl who had saved him.

"Who are you?" he called out into the night. But all he heard was the echo of his own voice.

"I'll be back soon," Ariel whispered as she and Flounder swam toward home. "Just wait and see. . . ."

Snow White
and the Seven Dwarfs

A Friend in Need

"Whatever could be keeping the Seven Dwarfs?" said Snow White. "It's getting late. They should have been home from the diamond mine by now!"

While she waited, Snow White busied herself tidying up their cottage in the woods. "What messy little fellows!" she said.

Just then, Happy came through the front door. He tugged on Snow White's long yellow skirt.

"Snow White," he said. "Come quickly! A young deer is hurt in the woods."

"Oh, no!" cried Snow White. "The poor thing! We must hurry!"

Soon they reached a small clearing. Everyone stood in a circle around the deer.

"Thank goodness you're here, Snow White!" said Doc. "This little fella's in trouble!"

"He must be cold," said Snow White, covering him with her long cape.

"Maybe he's just tired," said Sleepy, yawning. "A nice long rest should do the trick!"

"Why, you could be right, Sleepy," said Snow White. "But he's not closing his eyes, so I think it might be something else."

"Maybe he has a . . . aaahhhhh . . . aaahhhhhhh . . . chooooooooo . . . a cold," said Sneezy. "He looks like he might feel a bit stuffy."

"Well, that's possible. But then he probably would have stayed in his thicket until he was feeling better," said Snow White.

"I know!" said Happy. "Maybe he's feeling sad and needs a little cheering up!"

"I'm sure that would help, Happy," said Snow White. "But he looks like he may need something more than a merry story or a song."

"I, uh . . . don't know for sure," said Bashful softly. "But perhaps he's too shy to let us know what's the matter."

"We all feel shy sometimes, don't we, Bashful?" said Snow White.

Then Dopey started pacing back and forth and pointing over his shoulder.

"Hmm," said Snow White. "You could be right, Dopey. He could be lost."

"I'll bet I know what happened," grumbled Grumpy. "The wicked Queen probably cast a spell on him! She's always up to no good!"

Suddenly, Doc pushed his way past the others and approached the deer. "May I lake a took—er, I mean, take a look?" he asked, adjusting his eyeglasses.

Doc knelt down beside the deer.

"Well, would you look at that!" cried Doc. "The poor deer must have stepped on a thorn. Ouch!"

Doc gently removed the sharp thorn. The deer jumped up and licked him.

"Oh, how relieved you must be!" cried Snow White. "Now run along home," she said to their new friend. "Your family must be worried about you!"

The deer licked Snow White's hand and ran off into the forest.

Snow White and the Seven Dwarfs went home to their little cottage.

"I am so proud of each and every one of you," said Snow White, smiling at her friends. "You each did your best to help a friend in need!"

That night, Snow White and the Seven Dwarfs made a delicious dinner. Then when they'd all eaten their fill, they sang and danced until it was time for bed.

Jasmine

The Mysterious Voyage

Aladdin and Jasmine had just gotten married. People had come from near and far to celebrate. It had been the largest wedding in the history of Agrabah!

Now Aladdin and Jasmine were preparing to take a romantic trip far, far away.

"Abu, stay out of those bags!" warned Aladdin, smiling at his curious little friend. "That food is for our trip!

"Jasmine is going to be so surprised when she sees what I've planned!" said Aladdin as he finished packing. "She has lived most of her life within the walls of this palace. Now we're going to see the world . . . together!"

Soon Aladdin and Jasmine stood on the balcony, ready to begin their adventure.

"Madame, the Magic Carpet awaits you," said Aladdin, bowing before his new bride.

"Won't you tell me where we're going?" Jasmine asked as she took his hand. "I'm dying of curiosity."

"You are going to see things you've never ever seen before—a whole new, exciting world," Aladdin replied.

"Let's get going," said Jasmine. "I can't wait!"

Jasmine, Aladdin, and Abu settled onto the Magic Carpet. Then they took off, soaring high above the palace. Jasmine laughed with delight, the wind blowing her long hair behind her.

"Look how small everything looks!" she said. "It's like a dream."

After a little while, the Magic Carpet began its descent. "Are we there?" asked Jasmine.

"Almost," said Aladdin. "Close your eyes. I want this to be a surprise." Jasmine closed her eyes.

"No peeking!" Aladdin said.

Suddenly, the Magic Carpet landed on top of a high cliff. Jasmine heard a loud noise that sounded like crashing water.

"Can I open my eyes?" she asked excitedly.

"Okay. Open, sesame!" said Aladdin. "This, Jasmine, is the ocean!"

Jasmine couldn't believe her eyes. She had never seen anything so beautiful! The water was a brilliant shade of turquoise. Dolphins leaped in and out of the water as if they were dancing. Huge ocean waves crashed onto a white sandy beach in the distance.

"This is another world!" said Jasmine, her eyes shining happily. "I've read about the ocean, but I can't believe I'm actually seeing it with my own eyes. It's magical!"

They had a wonderful time swimming and enjoying the sun. When he and Jasmine were ready to go, Aladdin snapped his fingers. "Time for our next destination!" he said.

Within seconds, the Magic Carpet appeared. "I don't suppose you'll tell me what you've planned next," said Jasmine.

"That would ruin the surprise!" said Aladdin. "But I promise it will give you the chills."

Once again, Aladdin asked Jasmine to cover her eyes. As they descended, Jasmine felt the air grow colder. Suddenly she felt a warm coat hugging her shoulders.

"Okay, Jasmine," Aladdin said excitedly. "You can open your eyes now!"

This time, everywhere Jasmine looked, she saw white!

"Oh . . . what is it?" she asked, bending down to touch the cold white powder.

"It's snow!" answered Aladdin. "Isn't it wonderful? It falls from the sky when it's cold."

"It's amazing!" cried Jasmine. "It looks like a soft white cloud!

"Watch out!" she cried. Abu had thrown a snowball. It was heading straight for Aladdin.

They spent the rest of the day playing in the snow. They built snowmen and made snow angels. They even used the Magic Carpet as a sled to slide down a nearby hill over and over again.

Soon the sun began to set, and the air grew even colder.

"I think it's time to go!" said Aladdin. They climbed onto the Magic Carpet and took off.

"You've shown me places so different from Agrabah," said Jasmine happily. "There are plenty of brand-new worlds for us to share."

As they made their way back to the palace, Jasmine smiled. She knew that this was just the beginning of their wonderful life together.

THE LITTLE MERMAID

Ariel's Big Rescue

The news was traveling rapidly throughout the undersea world—a human ship had been spotted up on the surface not too far away.

"Flounder," Ariel said excitedly to her best friend. "Come on! Let's go look at the ship. Maybe we'll see some humans!"

"Uh, Ariel," Flounder began, "I don't think it's a good idea. Your father—"

"No, Flounder, listen," Ariel replied. "Daddy will never find out. And as for the humans, they won't see us if we just pop our heads above water for a minute. It'll be fine, honest!"

Soon Ariel and Flounder were swimming close to a large schooner.

"Look at it, Flounder!" Ariel exclaimed. "It must be a royal ship! It's so big!"

"Yeah, now let's get out of here, Ariel!" Flounder said shakily.

Ariel was thrilled as she swam to the surface. Sailors scurried about on deck.
A captain stood at the bow. And there was a girl . . . someone who looked like a
princess. Her braided black hair was gathered at the top of her head and had pearls
laced through it, and she wore a beautiful red dress.

Suddenly, the ship lurched, causing everyone aboard to stumble and fall. The sailors began scrambling about and shouting. A few minutes later, the captain approached the girl.

"Princess, I'm afraid I have some bad news," Ariel heard him say. "Nothing to worry about, but our ship has hit a reef and sprung a leak. Now, we're close enough to shore that we can make it. But I'm afraid we will have to toss extra items overboard to lighten the load. That will include your baggage, of course. Terribly sorry."

"Don't be sorry, Captain," the princess replied. "I'll do anything I can to help."

Ariel and Flounder quickly ducked below the surface.

"Let's take a look at that leak," Ariel said. "Maybe we can help."

As the two friends went under the ship, they noticed that it was not a small leak. There was a large hole in the hull, and water was rushing into the ship! The captain must have been trying to protect the princess by not letting her know how serious it was.

"Quick, Flounder!" Ariel said. "Gather all the seaweed you can! We'll stuff it into the hole. Maybe it will slow the leak enough to give them time to get to shore!"

Soon Ariel and Flounder were plugging the hole with kelp. Then they swam next to the ship as it started moving toward land. Their plan was working!

"Woo-hoo!" cried Flounder when the ship finally reached the shore. "We did it! They're going to make it!"

Relieved, Ariel poked her head above the surface and took one last look at the ship. How Ariel wished she could talk with the princess, just for a moment, to find out what it was really like to be human!

"We'd better go now, Flounder," she said, sighing.

But when she started swimming toward home, she gasped. There on the ocean floor was a trunk overflowing with honest-to-goodness, real human clothes. To Ariel, it was as good as a treasure chest!

"Flounder, this must be the princess's trunk!" she exclaimed. Hats, gloves, capes, corsets, jewelry—Ariel didn't know what they were called, but she tried on each and every one of them.

"Are you sure those holes are for your arms?" Flounder asked as Ariel struggled for a moment with a pair of frilly bloomers.

"Oh, yes, they must be!" She grinned. "They're so cute!"

Then Ariel pulled a long, blue gown out of the trunk. "I've never seen anything so beautiful!" she exclaimed.

Carefully, she held it up in front of her and smiled.

"Gee, Ariel, you look almost . . . human," Flounder said.

"I know." Ariel sighed. "Isn't it wonderful?"

Then she stopped. She thought of the human princess onshore, by now missing her lovely clothes and jewelry.

"You know, these things don't belong to me," Ariel said. "I should really return them to their rightful owner."

"Oh, no!" Flounder replied. "We're not going anywhere near those humans."

But that night, with Flounder by her side, Ariel took the trunk close enough to shore so that the tide could wash it up on the beach. Playing dress-up had been fun, but it felt much better to return the items to the princess.

"Maybe someday I'll be able to walk onshore and wear dresses just like hers," Ariel said dreamily. "I'll be a human princess, too—"

"Yeah, right," Flounder said. "And I'll be your king. Now, come on. Let's go home before we get into any more trouble!"

Jasmine

A Magical Surprise

It was a lovely day in Agrabah. The sun was shining brightly, with the gentlest of breezes drifting through the air. And in the garden of the palace, Princess Jasmine was pouring a bowl of tea for her pet Bengal tiger, Rajah.

It was, in fact, just like every other lovely day in Agrabah—and that was just the problem.

"Sorry to be so glum," Jasmine said to Rajah. "It's just that I was hoping to spend some time with Aladdin, but I can't seem to find him anywhere."

Rajah nodded his great, furry head sympathetically.

"To tell you the truth," Jasmine went on, "I'll bet Aladdin went off on the Magic Carpet today and completely forgot about me!"

Just then, to Jasmine's surprise, the Magic Carpet zoomed into the garden and stopped right in front of her—all alone. Jasmine watched it dart about and wave its tasseled corners, as if it were trying to tell her something. Clearly, Aladdin wasn't spending his day with the Magic Carpet!

"Whatever's wrong?" Jasmine asked it. "Where's Aladdin, Magic Carpet?" But when the Magic Carpet did a quick flip, Jasmine realized it wanted her to jump aboard for a ride. The Magic Carpet eagerly swooped down to pick her up, and soon Jasmine was riding high above land.

"Oh, Magic Carpet, it's beautiful up here," Jasmine said with a sigh. "But I'm worried about Aladdin."

Jasmine's thoughts began racing.

I hope Jafar hasn't somehow returned and locked him up! Or what if Aladdin's hurt himself and can't get help? she wondered.

"Magic Carpet, can you take me to Aladdin?" Jasmine asked. But the Magic Carpet didn't respond. Did the Magic Carpet not know where Aladdin was?

Taking matters into her own hands, Jasmine urged the Magic Carpet to go on a search for Aladdin. They rode over the desert, the marketplace, everywhere she could think of. Yet, nearly an hour later, they still had not found Aladdin.

At last, the princess told the Magic Carpet to return to the palace. Perhaps there they could get some more help.

Before long, the Magic Carpet landed with a bump right in the middle of the castle garden.

"SURPRISE!"

As Jasmine stood, dumbfounded, dozens of her friends and family leaped out from behind the bushes, carrying presents.

Delighted, Jasmine clapped her hands and smiled from ear to ear. But what was this all about? It wasn't her birthday—or any other special holiday for that matter.

Suddenly, Aladdin popped out from behind a large cake.

"Happy anniversary, Jasmine!" he said, beaming. "Are you surprised?"

"Surprised?" Jasmine replied. "Of course I am!" Then she added to Aladdin with a whisper, "It's not our anniversary!"

Aladdin smiled and whispered back, "It's the anniversary of the day we first met in the marketplace. I thought it was cause for a celebration."

Jasmine smiled and kissed Aladdin on the cheek. But when she looked at the Magic Carpet, she stopped abruptly. "Why, you sneaky thing!" she said. Then she smiled. "You were in on this surprise all along, weren't you?" She ruffled the Magic Carpet's tassels. Then she leaned in to whisper to it.

In an instant, the Magic Carpet swooped Aladdin and
Jasmine playfully up into the air and gave them an exciting ride
over the entire garden!

"Whoa!" cried Aladdin.

"Keep it up, Magic Carpet!" Jasmine shouted, laughing. Then she turned to Aladdin.
"This is what you get for scaring me like that."

"Hey, I'm sorry," Aladdin said. "I didn't mean to worry you. . . ."

"It's okay," she said with a smile. "This party, my friends and family—it's all wonderful."
This would certainly be a day the princess would never forget.

Snow White
and the Seven Dwarfs
A Royal Visit

Snow White was just about as happy as a princess could be. She lived in a beautiful castle—with a handsome and loving prince. She didn't have to worry about her wicked stepmother anymore. But, alas, she did miss one thing. . . .

"I've just been thinking about the Dwarfs," she said one day to the Prince. "It's been too long since I've seen them."

"Well, why don't we go pay them a visit?" the Prince suggested. "Their cottage is not so very far away."

Snow White's face instantly lit up. "But of course!" she said. "Let's go today!"

Sleepy was just waking up when a bluebird landed on the Dwarfs' windowsill.

"Say, there's a boat in his nose. Er—a note in his toes," said Doc, noticing the envelope in the bird's claws.

"Looks like a, uh . . . uh . . . ah . . . ah-*choo* . . . letter," said Sneezy.

"Indeed," said Doc. "But who would have sent it?"

Then he reached for the envelope, and the scent of sweet perfume drifted his way.

"Why, it's from Snow White!" Doc exclaimed.

"Achoo!" Sneezy sneezed.

"Well, stop sniffin' the durn thing and read it already," grumbled Grumpy.

"A-hem." Doc cleared his throat as the other Dwarfs eagerly waited.

"'My dear Dwarfs,'" Doc began. "Heh-heh, she calls us 'dear'!"

"Oh, get on with it," said Grumpy.

Doc scanned the note. "Well, um . . . well, golly gee! She's comin' for a visit! Today!" he cried. "At noon!"

"Hooray!" Happy cheered. "Snow White is coming!"

But the other six Dwarfs looked around their untidy cottage—at their unmade beds, their wrinkled clothes, and their dirty dishes piled high in the sink.

"She's comin' *today*?" Bashful gulped. "But we can't let her see the place lookin' like this!"

"And she's comin' at *noon*!" Grumpy huffed. "You know what that means, don'tcha? She'll want lunch. Someone's gonna have to cook!"

"Mmnnn . . . I'll need a nap," Sleepy said with a yawn.

"No naps and no more talkin'," Doc announced as he grabbed a broom. He handed it to Dopey. "We have a lot to do, men! Sleepy, you bake—er, *make* the beds. Bashful, you fold the clothes. Sneezy, you dust the furniture. Dopey will sweep the doors—er, *floors*. And Happy and Grumpy and I will fix somethin' suitable for Snow White to eat. Now, off to work we go! Go! Go!"

The Dwarfs started right away. But cooking and cleaning were not their strong points. Sleepy lay down in the middle of Grumpy's bed. Bashful hid behind a pile of clothes. Sneezy sneezed dust all around the room. And Dopey kept knocking things over with his broom.

As for Happy and Grumpy, they began to argue over what kind of sandwiches to make.

"Snow White likes peanut butter and jelly, I know," Happy declared.

"She likes ham and cheese," Grumpy grumbled.

By the time Doc finally got them to agree on something, the clock struck twelve and there was a soft rap upon the door.

"They're . . . ahh . . . ahh . . . *heeere*!" Sneezy sneezed. "Wake up, Sleepy!"

All at once, the Dwarfs ran up to open the door for their beloved princess, and they smiled as she hugged each and every one of them, then kissed them all on their foreheads.

"How I've missed you all!" she cried.

"Please, forgive the mess, Princess," Bashful whispered to her.

"Oh, Bashful," Snow White said with a laugh. "You must forgive *me* for giving you such short notice! Besides, I've come to see *you*—not your cottage."

"Would you care for a ham and jelly sandwich?" Doc offered. "Or peanut butter and cheese?"

"Oh, how sweet," Snow White kindly replied. "If I had known you'd go to all this trouble, I wouldn't have brought a picnic of my own."

"Picnic!" the Dwarfs exclaimed.

Just then, the Prince walked in with an overflowing basket.

"What's in it?" Doc asked hopefully.

"Oh, just some roast chicken and deviled eggs. Cinnamon bread and butter. Corn and tomatoes from the royal garden. Sugar cookies and a fresh apple pie . . . but let's eat your sandwiches first," said Snow White.

The Dwarfs looked at one another, and Doc cleared his throat.

"Nonsense, Princess," he told Snow White. "We can have ham and jelly any time. Let's enjoy the food you've brought. And you can tell us all about living happily after."

And that's exactly what they did.

Sleeping Beauty

The Wedding Gift

Sleeping Beauty had received True Love's Kiss at last. And now she was living happily back at the castle with her parents, preparing for the wonderful day when she would marry the man of her dreams, Prince Phillip.

Naturally, the whole castle was abuzz. The royal gardeners were gathering the

most fragrant flowers from the palace garden. The royal chefs were cooking up the grandest of wedding banquets. And the royal bakers were assembling a wedding cake tall enough to feed the entire kingdom.

And then there was the royal dressmaker, who, with her staff of twenty-two, had the most honored job of all—sewing the wedding dress of Princess Aurora's dreams.

The dressmaker curtsied to Aurora, her parents, and the three good fairies who had cared for Aurora for sixteen years.

"If you please, Your Royal Highness, what did you have in mind?" the dressmaker politely asked Aurora, as she held up samples to show the princess.

"Well," Aurora began, "I—"

"You'll want white, of course," the dressmaker broke in, "though not too white." She motioned to her assistants. "As Your Highness can see, I have some gorgeous ivory satin here. And an off-white brocade that's simply divine."

"Actually," Aurora said, "I—"

But the dressmaker wasn't done yet. "And by all means, you'll want a train! Twenty feet or so, I should say."

Truthfully, that wasn't what Aurora had had in mind at all. But before Aurora could say anything, the fairy Merryweather spoke up.

"But what if Briar Rose—oh, goodness me! I mean, Princess Aurora—doesn't want a dress that color?" she said, pointing to one of the samples.

Aurora smiled.

"What the dear girl needs is something *blue*," Merryweather said.

"Oh, no!" Flora scolded. "A wedding dress shouldn't be blue. It should be pink!"

Poor Aurora shook her head as she watched the fairies change the dress color.

"Or perhaps—" Fauna began.

"Just a minute now!" King Stefan declared, holding up his hand. "Pink, blue, ivory, or cream—I hereby decree that the color of the gown be left up to the bride."

Aurora sighed with relief and smiled as her father gave her shoulder a little squeeze.

Then the king went on. "The most important thing is that the dress be covered with *jewels*. Lots of them! After all, she *is* a princess!"

"Why, of course, Your Supreme Highness," the dressmaker said with a most reverent bow. "Lots of jewels. My thoughts exactly."

Aurora's face, once hopeful, suddenly fell. Jewels? Oh, dear. Wasn't that a little much?

While her father and the dressmaker discussed various bejeweled designs, Princess Aurora tried to think of the best way to tell them what kind of dress she herself wanted.

Then, suddenly, she felt a soft hand take hold of hers.

"Come, darling," her mother whispered, smiling. "I have something
I'd like to show you." She nodded toward the king and dressmaker, deep in
discussion. "I don't think they'll miss us for a few moments, do you?"

Together, the two walked up the stairs and into the Queen's dressing
room. There, Aurora watched her mother go to an old trunk, open it,
and pull out a long, beautiful gown, edged with delicate lace and tiny pearls.

"This was my wedding dress when I was a princess," the Queen explained. "And my mother's before me. I had hoped one day you'd wear it—if you'd like to, of course."

"Oh, Mother!" Aurora exclaimed. "It's just what I had in mind!"

Moments later, Aurora went back downstairs, wearing her mother's wedding gown.

"Oohh!" The fairies gasped.

"Ahh!" The dressmaker sighed.

"Perfect!" declared her father.

One and all agreed that the dress looked as if it had been made especially for Aurora—and, in a very special way, it had been.

Beauty and the Beast

Belle's Special Treat

"'And from that moment on, the princess had flowers every day of her life. The End,'" Belle read and closed the book with a sigh.

"What a treat!" she said to the Beast, as she gazed out of his library window at the cold, snowy hills. "The winter is lovely, of course . . . but to have flowers every day, I'd give anything. Wouldn't you?"

The Beast looked surprised. He had no idea Belle loved flowers that much. He had had so much else on his mind, after all. But he had also never seen this longing look in Belle's eyes. And the amazing thing was, he knew he could do something about it!

That evening, after Belle had gone to sleep, the Beast made his way to a part of his castle he hadn't visited in years—the royal greenhouse.

"Are we really going where I think we're going?" Lumiere the candelabrum asked with delight, as he lit the Beast's way.

But his master only nodded. All of a sudden, the Beast was worried. What if the flowers he'd once taken such pride in (*too* much pride, many had said) had died over time, from loneliness and neglect? They were, after all, rare and delicate species, collected from almost every corner of the world. And the Beast hadn't laid eyes on them since the day the enchantress had cast her spell on him and his castle. He just hadn't seen the point of caring for silly flowers—when no one would be coming to compliment them anymore.

What shape would they be in? he wondered.

Fortunately, the gardener (who was now a watering can) and his two assistants (transformed into a pair of clippers and a trowel) had watched over the greenhouse as best they could over the years. When the Beast walked in, he was pleased to see that his beloved flowers were still alive.

"There's still a lot of work to be done," he told Lumiere excitedly as he rolled up his sleeves and settled in to start working. But he knew he would enjoy every moment. And he did! He dug in the dirt, trimmed all sorts of plants, and pulled weeds. He tended his garden every day until it was back to its former glory.

One morning when Belle woke up, the first thing she saw was a big bouquet of daffodils—the earliest flowers of spring. "But it's still snowing outside," she said, utterly bewildered. "Wherever did these come from?"

Mrs. Potts just smiled. "Have a cup of tea, love," she said.

But Belle noticed that the Wardrobe, Mrs. Potts, and Chip were all smiling from ear to ear. Did they know something she didn't?

Throughout the day, Belle discovered flowers all over the castle. There were tulips in the dining room, lilies in the library, and six different colors of roses in the ballroom!

Finally, just as the sun was setting, Belle heard a knock on her door.

It was the Beast.

"Where have you been?" Belle asked. "I missed you."

"Really?" The Beast looked surprised.

"Really," Belle assured him. "And you've missed the most—"

Just then, Belle noticed there were leaves caught in the Beast's thick fur.

"Why, the flowers are from *you*!" she exclaimed.

"Oh, um . . ." the Beast answered gruffly. Then he added, "There's something I'd like to show you . . . that is, if you're willing."

"Of course," Belle said with a smile.

Eagerly, the Beast led Belle to the greenhouse. She gasped as she entered the room. The mountains of colorful blooms nearly took her breath away.

"I'd almost forgotten about this place," the Beast confessed. "That is, until you reminded me. Then I realized there *was* a way to have flowers every day."

"I really don't know how to thank you," Belle said, still amazed.

"Just enjoy them," the Beast told her. "If I'm not mistaken . . . that's what friends—and flowers—are for."